D0396953

For Newin on
His 6th Birthday
by
Tracy, Linae,
Bloz

The Banyan Deer

May All Beings
Be peaceful, Happy
and Free from Suffering
and Fear

Wisdom Publications
199 Elm Street
Somerville MA 02144 USA
www.wisdompubs.org

Text © 2010 Rafe Martin
Illustrations © 2010 Richard Wehrman
All rights reserved.
No part of this book may be reproduced in any form or by any means, elec-
tronic or mechanical, including photography, recording, or by any information storage and retrieval system or technologies now known or later
developed, without permission in writing from the publisher.

Library of Congress Cataloging-in-Publication Data available

14 13 12 11 10
5 4 3 2 1

Cover design by TLJB and Gopa&Ted2, Inc.
Interior design by Gopa&Ted2, Inc. Set in Perpetua Std 13/18.

Wisdom Publications' books are printed on acid-free paper and meet the
guidelines for permanence and durability of the Production Guidelines for
Book Longevity of the Council on Library Resources.

This book was produced with environmental mindfulness. We have elected
to print this title on 30% PCW recycled paper. As a result, we have saved
the following resources: 5 trees, 2 million BTUs of energy, 509 lbs. of greenhouse
gases, 2,451 gallons of water, and 149 lbs. of solid waste. For more information,
please visit our website, www.wisdompubs.org. This paper is also FSC certified.
For more information, please visit www.fscus.org.

Printed in the United States of America.

The Banyan Deer is a recreation of the traditional Buddhist
"Nigrodhamiga-jataka," a story of one of the Buddha's earlier
lifetimes, or "births." The original tale is No. 12 in the Pali
Jataka, a collection of 550 such stories.

The Banyan Deer

A Parable of Courage & Compassion

by Rafe Martin

Illustrated by Richard Wehrman

WISDOM PUBLICATIONS • BOSTON

"**M**OTHER**,**" said the young deer. "Is that King Banyan?"

"Yes, child. That is the king. His likeness was carved atop this stone pillar by order of a human king. And the story of this pillar is the story of how you were born."

"Me? My birth? Oh, please tell me the story!"

"That is why I brought you here. You are old enough now. We stand in the very spot it all took place.

"It was like this:

"Back when I still carried you within my body,
before you were born, that same human king I
mentioned loved to hunt."

"What did he hunt?" asked the young deer.

"He hunted animals, living creatures like us,"
answered his mother.

"Like us? But why?"

"He liked the chase. And he liked to eat meat."

"Meat?"

"Our bodies."

"Oh," said the young deer with a shudder.

"Yes, the king loved to hunt…"

...but the shopkeepers, teachers, wheelwrights, potters, tailors, carpenters, and farmers of his kingdom were not happy about it, not at all. For the king made all his subjects join him. He insisted that they help drive the forest animals toward his huntsmen's bows.

Because of this, fields lay idle. Children were not
well schooled. The potters' clay was not dug.
Tailors didn't cut and sew. Homes stood half built.

And so people decided to take matters into their own hands. To solve their problem they joined together and built a stockade deep in the forest. Then they drove two herds of deer inside. "Now," they said, "the king won't need us for his hunts. He can hunt whenever he wants, to his heart's content, and we can get back to our lives and work."

"And one of those herds was our herd?" asked the young deer. "And the Banyan Deer was our king?"

"Yes, one of the herds was our herd. But the Banyan Deer was not our king. Not then. He was the leader of the other herd."

"Oh," said the fawn with disappointment and confusion. "But isn't he our king?"

"Don't be sad," said the doe. "You're right. He is our king now. Listen to the story and you'll soon see for yourself what happened. All right?"

The fawn nodded, and so his mother went on...

The stockade gate was locked when the human king arrived. He climbed the steps to the top of the wall, looked down, and sighed, "How I will miss the glorious chase and the excitement of the hunt! But, yes, the people must have their lives. I will only shoot the deer in the stockade. You may all go back to your homes. Only my hunters need remain."

Then he added, "Those two deer kings, the leaders of the herds, are both magnificent animals. No one is to shoot them."

The people went home. The hunters shot a deer for the king's kitchen.

And to the king and his people, all seemed well.

But actually it was not. Not for us deer.

Many were wounded by flying arrows.

Many more were injured in the mad rush to escape the hunters' arrows.

And each day one of us was killed.

Every day it was the same.

The archers drew their bows and the stockade erupted in panic and chaos, each deer scrambling for safety. But there was no safety.

And each day another deer was carried off to the king's kitchen, while many other deer were hurt just trying to escape, just trying to stay alive.

One day the Banyan Deer went to the leader of
our herd. "Brother," he said, shaking his noble,
antlered head, "I have searched everywhere, tried
every exit, but there is no escape.

"So, for the sake of our herds, let us hold a lottery.
One day a deer from my herd will be selected by
lot to stand before the huntsmen, and the next day
a deer from yours. In this way, each day only one
deer will be shot and no others will be injured.

"It is a terrible solution, but at least in this way we
can relieve our peoples' suffering."

And our king agreed.

The next day, when the human king and his
bowmen came and stood atop the stockade wall,
they found one trembling deer standing there,
all alone.

The human king said, "Those deer kings are wise.
They have found a way to help their people."
I saw his face when he said it—
remember I, myself, was there.

And the human king looked troubled.

Then just one arrow flew,
and that one deer was killed.

But no other deer were injured.

And for many days that is how it went. Each day one deer died, and the rest were safe. Then one day the lot fell to a doe who was soon to give birth.

"Was that you, Mother?" asked the young deer.

"Yes," she answered, looking down tenderly at him. "It was. And the child I carried was you. But it wasn't right.

"The terms of the lottery were clear. Only one was supposed to die."

I went to my king and said, "Great King, the lot has fallen on me. But I am now with child. Once my fawn is born and able to live on its own, I will go willingly and take my place before the huntsmen. But if I go now, both I and my unborn fawn will die.

"The lottery claims only one life at a time. Please spare my child."

But my king said, "It's impossible. There can be no exceptions. The law is the law.

"The lottery fell on you, so now you must die."

"That was hard-hearted!" said the young deer, pawing the ground with his hoof. "He had been spared from the hunt and was never in any danger of losing his life. He should have spoken more kindly."

"Yes. That was my thought, too," said his mother.

"But I was not ready to give up yet. Instead, I ran to the Banyan Deer and told him of my troubles."

"You are right," said the Great Being. "You must wait till your fawn is born and strong enough to survive on its own. Go and be at peace.

"Another shall take your place."

Grateful beyond measure I bounded joyously away. But it was not just any deer who would die in my place.

No! It was the Banyan Deer King himself who now walked to where the hunters waited.

I had not understood that he meant to offer himself. But after all, how could he ask anyone else to make such a sacrifice? He had freed me, now he alone would take my place.

"That was very brave. He is a great king," said the young deer.

"The greatest," agreed the doe. "When I realized what he intended, I felt terrible. I hadn't meant for him to die. So I followed at a distance to watch what happened. Here's what I saw..."

When the hunters looked down, bows at the ready, they were shocked to see the great Banyan Deer himself standing below.

"Get the king," they called. When the human king came, the hunters said, "Sire, look!"

The king looked. "Banyan Deer King," he called in surprise. "Why have you come? You know I have spared you from my hunt. Go now and send another in your place."

"I cannot go. I have come here to take the place of a doe with fawn," said Great Banyan. "The lottery fell on her. But it is not right that two should die when our lottery only demands one. So I have taken her place."

The human king was amazed. "What?" he exclaimed. "You would give your own life to save another?"

"I would, Great King. I shall."

The human king was visibly shocked. He tugged at his beard and stared down at our noble Banyan Deer for a long, long time. Then at last he said, "Great Banyan Deer, this is a noble lesson. A king must care for the least of his subjects. I should learn from you. Such caring has not been my strength.

"So, in payment to you of a teacher's fee, I offer you a special gift. You and your herd can go free. Take your people and go live in peace. From this day forth you are all spared from my hunt."

But the great deer only shook his head. "O, King of Men, I cannot go," he said. "What of the other herd? If my herd and I now leave they will only suffer all the more, will they not?

"Day in and day out your arrows will only fall on them.

"What's more, the doe with fawn that I came here to save is in that herd. She and her unborn fawn would soon die once my herd and I left.

"What would be the point of buying our freedom at such a cost? How can I be free unless the other herd is free too?"

Seeing all this from my place of safety, I was stunned and filled with hope. My heart leapt with such fierce joy. The human king seemed astounded too.

Again he tugged his beard and stared down speechlessly into the stockade.

Then he said, "So, you would actually risk your safety and that of your herd, for this other herd, though they are none of your own?"

"I would, Great King," said the Banyan Deer. "I shall."

"This is a great lesson, indeed," admitted the human king. "Very great." He sighed deeply. "Then so shall it be. Go now and live in peace, for I shall free the other herd as well."

But the Banyan Deer did not leave. He again shook his head and said:

"Too long have I lived with danger to let it fall so heavily on others now. All the other four-footed animals of the forest will suffer terribly if I leave. They will be hunted without limit or mercy. How can I abandon them and be at peace myself, knowing that my freedom was bought at such a price? I know the terrors of the hunt. I, too, have lived in the midst of that fear. Free them as well, Great King—if you really mean for me to be happy and at peace, it is the only way."

The king hung his head and pondered.
Again, he sighed.

"It seems that you are determined to make crop farmers of us all! But I see your point. The wisdom of your words is clear. If you go, others will suffer all the more. So, what can I do? All the other animals shall be freed from my hunt as well.

"There. I am finished. It is done. You have been my teacher and now I feel that I have learned enough. The price of your wisdom is steep. But what you say is true. So, go and live in peace, Great Banyan King. You have freed the other herds and forest beasts."

It was very quiet.

I could hardly believe my ears.
We were all free!
I remember hearing a bird sing
from somewhere deep
in the forest.

It was a beautiful song.

But the Banyan Deer did not move.
He did not leave.

Instead he looked up at the trees and at the sky and said, "Alas, Sire, I cannot go. Your Majesty, look up! See the brightly feathered fliers that sing so sweetly and build their nests throughout your land. The birds, Sire, the birds! Your slings, nets, and arrows will now await them at every turn. Such a rain of death will fall upon them as could hardly be imagined.

"How can I leave and be at peace myself knowing this? Great King, have mercy. I beg you. Free them, too!"

I saw the king bite his lip. I saw him wipe his eyes.
At last he said, "Great Being, you are unrelenting
… but you are right.

"How can there be real peace unless it extends to
all? How can we be happy when any suffer?

"So now I release the birds, too, from my hunt.
From this day forth they shall fly freely
throughout my land. Go now, Great One, and at
last be at peace."

"Your Majesty," said the Banyan Deer, "in whom both wisdom and generosity overflow, how can I go?

"Your nets, hooks, and spears will soon be poised in terrible numbers above the silvery swimmers— the fish, Great King, the fish! Are they not beautiful? Do they not swirl and swim and leap, bringing life and beauty to every river, lake, and stream of your land? If I do not speak for these silent ones now, who ever will?

"How can I abandon them to such a fate? Let them live, too, Great King!"

"Are vegetables tasty when eaten alone?" asked the human king. "Are beans, grains, and fruit delicious when served without fish, fowl, or meat? For such now it seems must be my only food. You drive a hard bargain, Great Being. But, yes, again I see your wisdom. For any of us to have real peace, all beings—even the fish—must be free.

"Now hear this, all my courtiers and attendants!" announced the King. "From this day on, all living beings throughout my realm are to be held as my own dear subjects. None shall be hunted, none trapped or killed. All shall fall under my protection. This is my true wish and lasting decree."

Then, turning to the Banyan Deer, he said gently,
"There, Great One, are you now at peace?"

The Banyan Deer looked around and saw all us
deer grazing peacefully in the stockade. He looked
up and saw birds singing and soaring overhead.
Through spaces between the logs of the stockade,
he glimpsed the many forest animals.

A tear fell from the Deer King's eye—a single tear.
Yet in it was reflected the entire living world. "Yes,
Great King," he said. "Now I am at last at peace."
And he leapt like a fawn, leapt for joy, sheer joy.

He had saved us all!

"Open the gates!" called the human king, and the gates swung open.

Then the great Banyan Deer led both herds out of the stockade and back into the green forest.

When the herds separated and went their ways, I didn't hesitate a moment.

I went with the herd of the Banyan Deer.

Later, the human king had this pillar of stone set on the very spot where our Banyan Deer had made his great leap.

And on it he had carved this statue and these words:

PRAISE TO THE BANYAN DEER
TEACHER OF KINGS

"And so," said the doe, "I was the deer that Great Banyan saved. And you, my dear, were the unborn fawn whose life he spared."

"I was, wasn't I?" said the young deer slowly, taking it all in. "And it all began because I was about to be born. What a lucky event that was! And just in the nick of time, too! But, Mother… where did I ever come from?" asked the young deer.

"Why, you came from one of the heavens, no doubt," said his mother. "Because, if not for you, none of the deer, birds, fish, and animals would have been saved. Not one. If not—that is—for you and our Great Banyan Deer King."

"Imagine that," said the young deer.

"Yes," said the doe quietly. "Imagine it."